is a pet adopt-a-thon that has been held every year in New York City since 1998, when it was founded by Bernadette Peters and Mary Tyler Moore. Each summer, members of the Broadway acting community gather in the heart of New York's theater district to offer for adoption dogs and cats from local shelters. The event raises funds to help animal shelters and fosters awareness of the importance of caring for all the animals we keep as pets.

# BERNADETTE PETERS

# Broadway Barks

Pictures by
## LIZ MURPHY

Blue Apple Books

For Michael
—B.P.

For my husband, Tony
—L.M.

Special thanks to Michael Casey for introducing us
—H.M.Z. and B.P.

Thank you to Marvin Laird
for his musical arrangement of "Kramer's Song."
Thanks to Richard Hester, Patty Saccente
and, of course, Mary Tyler Moore.
—B.P.

All author royalties from this book
will be donated to "Broadway Barks."

Text copyright © 2008 by Bernadette Peters
Illustrations copyright © 2008 by Liz Murphy
All rights reserved / CIP Data is available.
Published in the United States 2008 by
Blue Apple Books, 515 Valley Street, Maplewood, N.J. 07040
www.blueapplebooks.com

Distributed in the U.S. by Chronicle Books
First Edition
Printed in China

ISBN: 978-1-934706-00-8

2 4 6 8 10 9 7 5 3 1

I used to be called Douglas.

I used to live in a tall apartment building.
But now I live in the park.

No one here knows my name.
I am waiting to be found.

No one takes me
for a walk.

No one gives me dinner.

And no one ever says,
"Good dog, Douglas."

I watch a lady
who is reading.
I hide.

She is pretty.
I'd like to sniff her hair.
Sometimes she hums.
I listen quietly.

I decide to follow the lady home.
But the streets are busy and I lose sight of her.

And I have to go back to the park.

The next day I see the lady again.
She is wearing party shoes.

I sit down next to her shoes.
She gives me a biscuit.
She gives me another.

Delicious!

When the pretty lady gets up
and walks down the path,
I follow the sweet smell
of biscuits.

The lady hails a taxi.
She turns and smiles at me, and I jump in.

To the taxi driver she says,
"Shubert Alley, please."

The cab ride is short.
When we get out of the taxi the lady tells me to sit.
I listen quietly while she talks.

THINK.

Today

BROADWAY Barks

"Here we are at *Broadway Barks*.
There will be a show.
Hopefully, someone from the audience
will adopt you and give you a good home."

We go backstage.
Someone ties a scarf around my neck.

There are many other dogs.
And cats too.
I am very nervous.
I am going to be on the stage.

I watch from the side.

# THE SHOW BEGINS!

A tall lady with a pretty smile
starts the show.
"Welcome to *Broadway Barks*.
We have wonderful dogs and cats
waiting for you to give them
good homes."

Everyone claps and cheers.

I hear singing.

Then it's my turn.

I sing.

Everyone laughs.
They just hear barking.

Then
I dance.

Everyone laughs harder.
They just see jumping.

Someone grabs my leash
and pulls me offstage.

I'm alone.

No one loves me. Nobody wants me.

Suddenly, out of nowhere,
a small girl appears.

She says,
"I loved your singing.
I loved your dancing.
Would you like to go home with me?"

I smile, "Yes!"
The girl hugs me.
She smells good.

Then she says, "My name is Isabel.
You look like a Kramer to me.
From now on I'm going to call you Kramer."

At my new house, I am given dinner . . .

KRAMER

a bath...

and a belly rub.

When I do
a little dance after dinner,
I hear,

"Good dog, Kramer."

In Isabel's room
there's a nice
cozy bed
for me to sleep in.

Isabel sings me to sleep.

"Good night, my pal.
Good night, my friend.
Tomorrow I'll see you again."

Good night, Kramer. Good night, Isabel.